ASTERIX THE LEGIONARY

TEXT BY GOSCINNY

DRAWINGS BY UDERZO

TRANSLATED BY ANTHEA BELL AND DEREK HOCKRIDGE

HODDER DARGAUD
LONDON SYDNEY AUCKLAND

ASTERIX IN OTHER COUNTRIES

Australia	Hodder Dargaud, Rydalmere Business Park, 10/16 South Street, Rydalmere, N.S.W. 2116, Australia
Austria	Delta Verlag GmbH, Postfach 10 12 45, 7000 Stuttgart 10, Germany
Belgium	Dargaud Benelux, 17 Avenue Paul Henri Spaak, 1070 Brussels, Belgium
Belorussia	c/o Egmont Lithuania, Juozapaviciaus 9 A, Room 910/911, Vilnius, Lithuania
Brazil	Record Distribuidora, Rua Argentina 171, 20921 Rio de Janeiro, Brazil
Bulgaria	Egmont Bulgaria Ltd., Ul. Sweta Gora 7, IV et., 1421 Sofia, Bulgaria
Canada	*(French)* Presse-Import Leo Brunelle Inc., 371 Deslauriers St., St. Laurent, Quebec H4N 1W2, Canada
	(English) General Publishing Co. Ltd., 30 Lesmill Road, Don Mills, Ontario M38 2T6, Canada
Croatia	Izvori Publishing House, Trnjanska 47, 4100 Zagreb, Croatia
Czech Republic	Egmont CSFR, Hellichova 45, 118 00 Prague 1, The Czech Republic
Denmark	Serieforlaget A/S (Egmont Group), Vognmagergade 11, 1148 Copenhagen K, Denmark
Estonia	Egmont Estonia Ltd., Tartu Mnt. 16, Building A, 3rd Floor, Tallinn EE 0105, Estonia
Finland	Sanoma Corporation, P.O. Box 107, 00381 Helsinki 38, Finland
France	Dargaud Editeur, 6 Rue Gager-Gabillot, 75015 Paris, France
	(titles up to and including Asterix in Belgium)
	Les Editions Albert René, 26 Avenue Victor Hugo, 75116 Paris, France
	(titles from Asterix and the Great Divide onwards)
Germany	Delta Verlag GmbH, Postfach 10 12 45, 7000 Stuttgart 10, Germany
Greece	*(Ancient and Modern Greek)* Mamouth Comix Ltd., 44 Ippokratous St., 106080 Athens, Greece
Holland	Dargaud Bénélux, 17 Avenue Paul Henri Spaak, 1070 Brussels, Belgium
	(Distribution) Betapress, Burg. Krollaan 14, 5126 PT Jilze, Holland
Hong Kong	*(English)* Hodder Dargaud, c/o Publishers Associates Ltd., 11th Floor, Taikoo Trading Estate, 28 Tong Cheong Street, Quarry Bay, Hong Kong
	(Mandarin and Cantonese) Gast, Flat C, 5/F, Block 3, Site 1, Whampoa Garden, Hunghom KLN, Hong Kong
Hungary	Egmont Hungary Kft., Fészek utca 16 B, 1125 Budapest, Hungary
Indonesia	Penerbit Sinar Harapan, Jl. Dewi Sartika 136D, Jakarta Cawang, Indonesia
Italy	Mondadori, Via Belvedere, 37131 Verona, Italy
Republic of Korea	Cosmos Editions, 19-16 Shin An-dong, Jin-ju, Gyung Nam-do, Republic of Korea
Latin America	Grijalbo-Dargaud, Aragon 385, 08013 Barcelona, Spain
Latvia	Egmont Latvia Ltd., Balasta Dambis 3, Room 1812, 226081 Riga, Latvia
Lithuania	Egmont Lithuania, Juozapaviciaus 9 A, Room 910/911, Vilnius, Lithuania
Luxemburg	Imprimerie St. Paul, rue Christophe Plantin 2, Luxemburg
New Zealand	Hodder Dargaud, P.O. Box 3858, Auckland 1, New Zealand
Norway	A/S Hjemmet - Serieforlaget, PB 6853 St. Olavs pl. 0130 Oslo, Norway
Poland	Egmont Polska Ltd., Plac Marszalka J. Pilsudskiego 9, 00-078 Warsaw, Poland
Portugal	Meriberica-Liber, Avenida Duque d'Avila 69, R/C esq., 1000 Lisbon, Portugal
Roman Empire	*(Latin)* Delta Verlag GmbH, Postfach 10 12 45, 7000 Stuttgart 10, Germany
Russia	Egmont Russia, Apt. 123, Narodmaya Ulitsa 13, 1091172 Moscow, Russia
Serbia	Nip Forum, Vojvode Misica 1-3, 2100 Novi Sad, Serbia
Slovak Republic	Egmont Neografia, Nevädzova 8, Box 20, 827 99 Bratislava 27, The Slovak Republic
Slovenia	Didakta, Radovljica Kranjska Cesta 13, 64240 Radovljica, Slovenia
South Africa	Hodder Dargaud, c/o Struik Book Distributors (Pty) Ltd., Graph Avenue, Montague Gardens 7441, South Africa
Spain	*(Castillian and Catalan)* Grijalbo-Dargaud, Aragon 385, 08013 Barcelona, Spain
Sweden	Serieförlaget Svenska AB (Egmont Group), 212 05 Malmö, Sweden
Switzerland	Dargaud (Suisse) S.A., En Budron B, Le Mont sur Lausanne, Switzerland
USA	*(English and French)* Presse-Import Leo Brunelle Inc., 371 Deslauriers St., St. Laurent, Quebec H4N 1W2, Canada

Asterix the Legionary

ISBN 0 340 10392 2 (cased)
ISBN 0 340 18321 7 (limp)

First published in Great Britain 1970 (cased)
This impression 93 94 95 96 97

First published in Great Britain 1974 (limp)
This impression 93 94 95 96 97

Published by Hodder Dargaud Ltd,
Mill Road, Dunton Green, Sevenoaks, Kent TN13 2YA

Printed in Belgium by Proost International Book Production

ıe year is 50 BC. Gaul is entirely occupied by the Romans. ell, not entirely... One small village of indomitable Gauls still olds out against the invaders. And life is not easy for the oman legionaries who garrison the fortified camps of otorum, Aquarium, Laudanum and Compendium...

a few of the Gauls

Asterix, the hero of these adventures. A shrewd, cunning little warrior; all perilous missions are immediately entrusted to him. Asterix gets his superhuman strength from the magic potion brewed by the druid Getafix...

Obelix, Asterix's inseparable friend. A menhir delivery-man by trade; addicted to wild boar. Obelix is always ready to drop everything and go off on a new adventure with Asterix – so long as there's wild boar to eat, and plenty of fighting.

Getafix, the venerable village druid. Gathers mistletoe and brews magic potions. His speciality is the potion which gives the drinker superhuman strength. But Getafix also has other recipes up his sleeve...

Cacofonix, the bard. Opinion is divided as to his musical gifts. Cacofonix thinks he's a genius. Everyone else thinks he's unspeakable. But so long as he doesn't speak, let alone sing, everybody likes him...

Finally, Vitalstatistix, the chief of the tribe. Majestic, brave and hot-tempered, the old warrior is respected by his men and feared by his enemies. Vitalstatistix himself has only one fear; he is afraid the sky may fall on his head tomorrow. But as he always says, 'Tomorrow never comes.'

THE SUN IS SHINING, AND ALL IS QUIET IN THE LITTLE GAULISH VILLAGE WE KNOW SO WELL...
NICE DAY, OBELIX! LET'S MAKE THE MOST OF IT! HOW ABOUT A BOAR HUNT?
GOOD IDEA ASTERIX!
WOOF!

BOOM!
CRAAASH!
?!?
OUCH!

ENJOYING YOURSELF, OBELIX, PUSHING TREES OVER WHILE I'M UP IN THEM CUTTING MISTLETOE?

WELL...ER...WELL, IT'S AN UNTIDY SORT OF FOREST ANYWAY. TREES ALL OVER THE PLACE!

RIGHT! ARE WE GOING ON THIS HUNT?

!?!
HOWWWL!

LATER...
GOOD HUNTING, OBELIX, EH?
HMMM?

LET'S GO AND COOK THE BOARS RIGHT AWAY. THEN WE CAN HAVE A NICE REST!

HEY, OBELIX! WHERE ARE THOSE BOARS?

MMPH... BOARS? WHAT BOARS?

OH, YOU MEAN THESE BOARS...
GRRRRRRRRR!

SOON AFTERWARDS...
AAAH! THAT WAS GOOD!
2A

NOW THEN, OBELIX, EAT UP YOUR THIRD BOAR. THEN WE'LL HAVE OUR REST
NO, THANKS. SOMEHOW I DON'T FEEL HUNGRY ANY MORE-DEEP SIGH
SCROTCH SCRUTCH

OBELIX! ARE YOU ILL?
NO, NO.... DEEPER SIGH

DEEPEST SIGH

COME QUICK, O DRUID GETAFIX! I'M WORRIED! OBELIX WON'T EAT UP HIS BOAR. HE SAYS HE DOESN'T FEEL HUNGRY!
DID HE HAVE ANYTHING ELSE FIRST?

JUST TWO BOARS
TWO BOARS...THAT HARDLY COUNTS. BETTER HAVE A LOOK AT HIM!
2B

HE KEEPS BUMPING INTO TREES, HE WON'T EAT, HE LET TWO ROMANS AND A BOAR GO...

GOOD AFTERNOON, O DRUID GETAFIX!
AFTERNOON...

NOW SPEAKING OF BOARS...

!?

WHERE ARE YOU GOING, OBELIX?
CLICK!
EH? ME? I'M DELIVERING MENHIRS!

MENHIRS? BUT YOU HAVEN'T GOT ANY MENHIRS!
SO I HAVEN'T... WELL, I COULD HAVE SWORN I HAD THEM WHEN I STARTED OUT
SCRATCH! SCRATCH!
3A

PANACEA! COME HERE A MINUTE!

YES, O DRUID?
PANACEA, HAVE YOU MET ASTERIX AND OBELIX?

PANACEA! YOU'RE SOPORIFIX'S DAUGHTER... THE ONE WHO WENT TO STUDY AT CONDATUM*... YOU **HAVE** CHANGED!
I'VE BEEN AT CONDATUM FOR TWO YEARS. WHEN I WENT AWAY I WAS JUST A LITTLE GIRL WITH MY HAIR IN PIGTAILS
* RENNES

YOU REMEMBER OBELIX?
OF COURSE I DO! THE ONE WHO FELL IN THE POTION WHEN HE WAS A BABY! HOW ARE YOU, OBELIX?
WKRSTKSFT

AND THIS IS DOGMATIX
ISN'T HE SWEET!
GRRRRR!

3B
GOODBYE!

!?!?

HAHAHA!
HOHOHO!
HEEHEE!
CLICK!

HEEHEEHEEHEE! HOHO! HOHO!
WHAT'S UP WITH YOU?

MY DEAR OBELIX, YOU'RE IN LOVE!
WHO, ME? HUH!

WHETHER DOGMATIX LIKES IT OR NOT!
HUH

I DON'T HAVE ANY MAGIC POTION FOR THAT!
HA! HUMPH!
4A

BETWEEN YOU AND ME, YOU LIKE LITTLE PANACEA, DON'T YOU?
WELL, I... ER...
BONG! BONG! BONG!

WHY DON'T YOU GO AND SEE HER? SOPORIFIX'S HUT IS QUITE NEAR.
OOH, I COULDN'T!

I COULDN'T!
CRAASH!

HOWWWL!
BUT I WASN'T EVEN SINGING!
4B

YOU OUGHT TO GIVE PANACEA A LITTLE PRESENT, TO WELCOME HER HOME...
SNIFF!

IT WOULD GIVE YOU THE CHANCE TO GET INTO CONVERSATION WITH HER, TOO!
THAT'S A GOOD IDEA! THAT'S A VERY GOOD IDEA! YES, THAT'S IT... I'LL GO AND FIND A PRESENT!
TAP! TAP! TAP! TAP!

YOU KNOW THE FORM, ASTERIX!
HA!

THERE!
!?!

YOU'RE NEVER GOING TO GIVE HER THAT??
WHY NOT? IT'S THE VERY BEST I'VE GOT IN STOCK!
5A

BUT THAT'S NO PRESENT TO GIVE A GIRL!
WELL, WHAT IS, THEN? A DOLMEN? A BOAR?

NO, NO! YOU WANT TO GIVE HER SOMETHING DELICATE, POETIC... FLOWERS, THAT'S IT! FLOWERS! YOU WANT TO GO AND PICK HER A NICE BUNCH OF FLOWERS IN THE FOREST. SHE'D LIKE THAT!

THAT'S A GOOD IDEA! I'M OFF!

AND WATCH OUT! DON'T GO BUMPING INTO ANY TREES!
HUH!

AT THIS VERY MOMENT, IN ANOTHER PART OF THE FOREST, A ROMAN PATROL IS ADVANCING CAUTIOUSLY, BY JUPITER...
AND WATCH OUT! MIND YOU DON'T GO BUMPING INTO ANY GAULS!
5B

I KNOW A SPOT NEAR THE BIG OAK WHERE THERE ARE LOTS OF PRETTY FLOWERS. DELICATE POETIC BLUE FLOWERS

THERE'S SOMEONE COMING, BY MERCURY! IT MAY BE THE GAULS! LET'S TRY AND GET BY WITHOUT BEING NOTICED!
OVER THERE! BY THAT BIG OAK!

I... I THINK THEY'RE COMING THIS WAY!

6A

ER...QUOMODO VALES?
AREN'T YOU ASHAMED OF YOURSELVES, TREADING ON MY PRETTY BLUE FLOWERS?

WE'RE TERRIBLY SORRY... WE DIDN'T KNOW WE HAD TO KEEP OFF THE...

WHAM!

AND HAVING GOT RID OF THE INTRUDERS...
THE TROUBLE WITH YOU ROMANS IS, YOU AREN'T DELICATE OR POETIC...

AND THE TROUBLE WITH ME IS, I'M SO SHY AND RETIRING!
SNIFF!

HEAR WHAT THAT MASTODON SAID?
IF YOU ASK ME, THESE GAULS ARE CRAZY!
6B

THAT'S A NICE LITTLE BUNCH OF FLOWERS. VERY POETIC...

WOULDN'T IT BE EVEN MORE POETIC IF I PUT IT IN A HELMET?
NO, NO! PUT YOUR HELMETS DOWN AND TAKE THE FLOWERS TO PANACEA

OO, I COULDN'T... YOU COME WITH ME!
IF YOU LIKE!

YOU COMING TOO, DOGMATIX?
HUH!

YOU GIVE HER THE FLOWERS, ASTERIX. I'LL BE OFF NOW...
YOU JUST STAY THERE!

PANACEA!
SSH! SHE MIGHT HEAR YOU!

HELLO, ASTERIX!
PANACEA, MY FRIEND OBELIX HAS A PRESENT FOR YOU...

A PRESENT FOR ME?
THAT'S RIGHT, A PRESENT FOR YOU
GO ON, GIVE HER THE FLOWERS!
POM! POM! POM!

OH, WHAT PRETTY FLOWERS!

LET'S SIT DOWN HERE A MINUTE...
SAY SOMETHING!
WGHSTRFG...

RIGHT, THEN, I'LL BE OFF

A MESSAGE FOR YOU, PANACEA!
HULLO! THAT'S POSTALDISTRIX THE POSTMAN!

YOU DON'T MIND IF I READ IT NOW?
NOT AT ALL!

OH! BY BELISAMA!

WHAT'S THE MATTER? IS IT BAD NEWS?
READ THAT!

I'VE JUST GOT TIME TO CARVE A WORD. THE ROMANS MADE ME JOIN THE LEGION. WE'RE OFF TO AFRICA. FAREWELL FOR EVER
TRAGICOMIX

WHO'S TRAGICOMIX, PANACEA?
WE GOT TO KNOW EACH OTHER AT CONDATUM. WE'RE ENGAGED...

DON'T CRY, PANACEA. WE'LL GO AND FIND TRAGICOMIX FOR YOU. WON'T WE, ASTERIX?

I'LL SAY! WE'LL BRING HIM BACK EVEN IF WE HAVE TO GO ALL THE WAY TO AFRICA! LET'S GO AND SEE OUR CHIEF VITALSTATISTIX, OBELIX!

OBELIX, I'M PROUD OF YOU! YOU WERE REALLY BRAVE! WHEN YOU HEARD PANACEA WAS ENGAGED YOU DIDN'T EVEN...

BOOHOOHOOOO! I'M SO UNHAPPY!

SNIFF
THIS IS ODD, O VITALSTATISTIX. WHY HAVE THE ROMANS TAKEN TO RECRUITING GAULS?
JULIUS CAESAR'S IN TROUBLE IN AFRICA. HE'S OUT THERE FIGHTING THE ROMANS WHO SUPPORT POMPEY...
HUH!

ACCORDING TO THE LATEST NEWS, HE'S BESIEGED IN RUSPINA*. HE NEEDS REINFORCEMENTS. HIS RECRUITING OFFICERS GO AROUND ASKING FOR VOLUNTEERS, AND WHEN THEY DON'T GET THEM THEY TAKE THEM BY FORCE...
*MONASTIR (TUNISIA)

WE'LL GO TO CONDATUM AT ONCE TO TRY AND GET YOUNG TRAGICOMIX BACK BEFORE HE LEAVES FOR AFRICA!

THAT'S EXACTLY WHAT I THOUGHT YOU'D SAY! IT JUST SHOWS YOUR INDOMITABLE COURAGE! PANACEA'S FIANCÉ...

BOOHOOHOOO!

PREPARATIONS FOR THE JOURNEY ARE QUICKLY MADE...
HERE'S SOME MAGIC POTION FOR YOU, ASTERIX
THANKS, O DRUID GETAFIX!
SNIFF!

...AND IT IS TIME TO LEAVE
HOW CAN I EVER THANK YOU?
YOU CAN THANK US WHEN WE BRING TRAGICOMIX BACK – AND BRING HIM BACK WE WILL, UNLESS THE SKY FALLS ON OUR HEADS!
BE A GOOD LITTLE DOG, DOGMATIX. I'LL BE BACK SOON...

I'D LIKE YOU TO LOOK AFTER DOGMATIX, PANACEA
I'LL TAKE CARE OF HIM, OBELIX... ISN'T HE SWEET!
GRRRR!

SMACK!

OH, SO I'M NOT GOING TO SING ?
NO, YOU ARE NOT GOING TO SING !

AFTER A SHORT AND UNEVENTFUL JOURNEY...
WE'VE GOT TO FIND THE ROMAN H.Q. AS SOON AS WE SEE A LEGIONARY WE'LL ASK HIM THE WAY
CONDATVM

AND NOT FAR AWAY, IN THE STREETS OF CONDATUM...
HEY, YOU! WHY AREN'T YOU SALUTING THE PATROL?
AVE!

AVE!
WE'LL SAY NO MORE ABOUT IT THIS TIME...JUST REMEMBER, ALWAYS SALUTE THE PATROL!
LOOK, THERE'S A PATROL! WE'LL JUST STOP IT AND...

RIGHT!
OBELIX! WAIT A MINUTE!

SEVERAL MINUTES LATER...
WE ONLY NEEDED TO STOP THEM!
WELL, WE HAVE STOPPED THEM!

THERE ARE TIMES WHEN IT PAYS TO BE POLITE, OBELIX...

WOULD YOU BE SO KIND AS TO DIRECT ME TO YOUR HEAD-QUARTERS, PLEASE?
THIRD ON THE LEFT, AND PLEASE DON'T HIT ME ANY MORE!

POLITENESS WILL GET YOU EVERYWHERE, OBELIX...
AVE

AH, HERE'S THE LEGION HEADQUARTERS... YOU WAIT FOR ME HERE. I DON'T TRUST YOU. WE HAVE TO BE POLITE

NO ENTRY! IF YOU WANT TO JOIN UP, GAUL, WAIT IN LINE LIKE EVERYONE ELSE
I'M TERRIBLY SORRY... ..I ONLY WANTED SOME INFORMATION

GET IN LINE, I SAID!
THE FACT IS, I'M IN A BIT OF A HURRY!

NOTHING TO DO WITH ME!
THIS IS GETTING ME DOWN! THIS REALLY IS GETTING ME DOWN, BY TOUTATIS!

BIFF!

REALLY!

HONESTLY, I DON'T SEE ANY DIFFERENCE BETWEEN ASTERIX'S POLITENESS AND MINE!
TCHAC!

WHERE DO I FIND THE INFORMATION BUREAU, PLEASE ?
NO IDEA. APPLY TO THE INFORMATION BUREAU. THEY'LL INFORM YOU
11

INFORMATION
AH, AT LAST!

PLEASE COULD YOU TELL ME IF YOU HAVE A LEGIONARY HERE BY THE NAME OF TRAGICOMIX?
STOP CARVING THAT OUT, ERRONEUS, WE CAN'T HEAR OURSELVES SPEAK!
TAPTAPTAPTAP!

APPLY TO THE PERSONNEL DEPARTMENT. FOURTH DOOR ON THE LEFT

PERSONNEL DEPARTMENT...
DEPLOYMENT OF FORCES
FOUR EMPRESSES!
APPLY TO THE CENTURION OF CALENDS, GAUL...

12A

WE'RE GOING TO HANG OUT OUR WASHING ON THE CATILINE...
CENTURION OF CALENDS

OH NO, YOU WANT THE INFORMATION BUREAU, BY JUPITER...

INFORMATION
I'VE HAD JUST ABOUT ENOUGH OF THIS!
BANG!

ARE YOU GOING TO TELL ME WHERE TRAGICOMIX IS OR AREN'T YOU?
TAPTAPTAPTAP!
BIFF! BIFF! BIFF! BIFF! BIFF!

STOP CARVING HIM UP, GAUL, WE CAN'T HEAR OURSELVES THINK!
BIFF! BIFF! BIFF!
12B

I'M RIGHT IN THE MIDDLE OF CARVING OUT THE LIST OF VOLUNTEER RECRUITS TO BE ISSUED TO ALL DEPARTMENTS ... THERE HAVE TO BE TWELVE COPIES. WHAT WAS THE NAME AGAIN ?

TRAGICOMIX
TRAGICOMIX ... WITH A "T", AS IN TIMEO DANAOS ET DONA FERENTES ?

AH, HERE WE ARE ... TRAGICOMIX HAS LEFT WITH A CONVOY. AT THIS MOMENT HE'S DUE TO TAKE SHIP AT MASSILIA WITH REINFORCEMENTS FOR CAESAR. THEY'RE OFF TO AFRICA

AFRICA ... HMMM ...

OBELIX ! COME HERE !

IS THAT YOU, ASTERIX ?
YES !
13A

COMING !

NOW THEN ! LET'S BE POLITE !
WHAM !
?!!

TRAGICOMIX HAS LEFT FOR AFRICA. THE ONLY WAY TO GET HIM BACK NOW IS TO JOIN THE ROMAN ARMY
WHAT, US ? JOIN THE ROMAN ARMY ? STILL, IF YOU THINK IT WOULD HELP PANACEA ..

SOON AFTERWARDS ...
OUCH ... WHAT DID THOSE TWO HAVE AGAINST ME, ANYWAY ... ?

13B

AH, HERE ARE THE VOLUNTEERS! COME ALONG IN, YOUNG FELLOWS. PLEASED TO MEET YOU
POC!

WE WEREN'T PARTICULARLY POLITE THAT TIME, ASTERIX
THERE'S A TIME AND A PLACE FOR EVERYTHING, OBELIX

SPLENDID, BOYS, SPLENDID! YOU WILL NOW GIVE YOUR NAMES TO THE LEGIONARY. HE WILL CARVE YOU DOWN...
14A

NEVERATALOS, GREEK, BY ZEUS!
SELECTIVEMPLOYMENTAX, BRITISH, I SAY, WHAT!
GASTRONOMIX, BELGIAN

Hemispheric, Gothic!
Allegoric, Gothic!
INTERPRETER?
HEMISPHERIC AND ALLEGORIC. THEY'RE GOTHS

HE WANTS TO KNOW IF THIS REALLY IS AN INN?
TELL HIM YES, AND ASK HIM FOR HIS NAME FOR THE REGISTER

PTENISNET
TOC TOC TOC!

ASTERIX AND OBELIX, GAULS
AND THAT'S THE LOT!
TOC TOC TOC!
SILENCE! STOP GIGGLING! YOU'RE IN THE ARMY NOW!
14B

GET INTO LINE! AND JUMP TO IT!
YOU WANT ME TO BE POLITE TO HIM, ASTERIX?
NOT JUST YET, OBELIX

SILENCE!

WHAT'S HE SAYING?
HE SAYS HE WANTS A ROOM LOOKING ON TO THE STREET

LOOK, ARE WE GOING TO KEEP TALKING LIKE THIS MUCH LONGER? THE FACT IS, WE'RE IN A HURRY
WHAT!? IF I FEEL LIKE TALKING, MY LITTLE FRIEND...

SIIILENCE!

What's going on around here?
TOC TOC TOC
The Egyptian wants a room looking on to the street
Can we choose our rooms, then?
LET'S ALL JUST KEEP CALM...

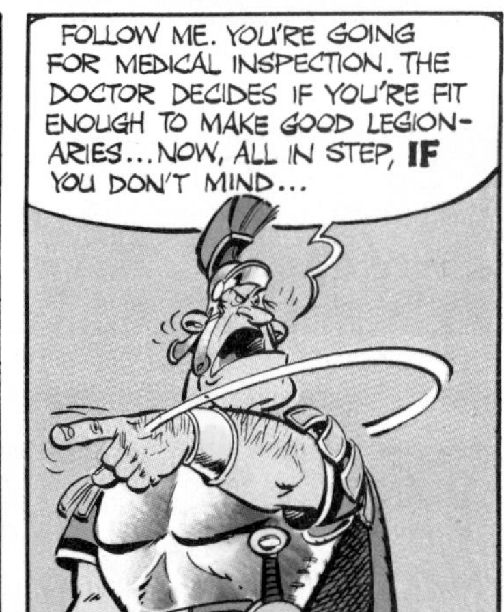
FOLLOW ME. YOU'RE GOING FOR MEDICAL INSPECTION. THE DOCTOR DECIDES IF YOU'RE FIT ENOUGH TO MAKE GOOD LEGIONARIES... NOW, ALL IN STEP, IF YOU DON'T MIND...

ONE, TWO! ONE, TWO! ONE...
CENTURION! THE EGYPTIAN SAYS HE WANTS ONE, NOT TWO, BUT IT MUST LOOK ON TO THE STREET

WHERE...WHERE WAS I?
YOU'D GOT TO ONE...
I THINK TWO COMES NEXT

HERE ARE THE NEW RECRUITS
RIGHT. TELL THEM TO GET UNDRESSED

U-UN-DRESS!
Undress!

Too skinny for a legionary, he said!

I don't make the weight, he said!
DOCTO

THE EGYPTIAN FINDS THE CUSTOMS OF GAULISH INNS RATHER SURPRISING. HE SAYS...
I DON'T CARE WHAT HE SAYS! HE'S GOOD ENOUG FOR CAESAR EVERYONE OUT!

NOW YOU GET DRESSED!
I WISH YOU'D MAKE UP YOUR MIND!
THESE ROMANS ARE CRAZY!
What did the Gaul say?
He said the centurion can't make up his mind!

WHO ASKED YOU TO TRANSLATE?

What did the centurion say?
WHAT DID THE GOTH SAY?

SO YOU DO WANT ME TO TRANSLATE?

GNGNGNGNGNGNGNGN
LISTEN, WE'RE NOT HERE FOR THE FUN OF IT! TELL US WHERE WE'RE SUPPOSED TO GO. HOW ABOUT A BIT OF ROMAN LAW AND ORDER?

THIS IS WHERE YOU GET YOUR UNIFORM...
THERE ARE THREE SORTS: SMALL, MEDIUM AND LARGE. CALL OUT YOUR SIZES!

SMALL
THERE YOU ARE

MEDIUM
?!!

DON'T BE SO SILLY, OBELIX
WHAT DO YOU MEAN? I DON'T WEIGH MUCH. LOOK...
?

GNGNGNGN!

WHAT IS IT THIS TIME?

BIFF!
BZOINNNG!

ARE YOU QUITE SURE THAT ONE WAS MEDIUM?
I DON'T KNOW WHAT YOU WEIGH, BUT THAT'S NO WAY TO PLEASE THE CENTURION!

What did the centurion say?
He said

WHAT DID YOU SAY TO HIM?

I SAY, SINCE WE'RE TALKING ABOUT THAT KIND OF THING, DID YOU HEAR THE ONE ABOUT THE BRITON, THE HIBERNIAN AND THE CALEDONIAN...

BONG! BONG! BONG!
NOW WE'RE GOING DOWN TO THE COURTYARD FOR A LITTLE TRAINING

WAIT A MINUTE! WE HAVEN'T FIXED OUR PAY YET!
?!!

TWO AND A HALF SESTERTII, I SAID!
YOU MUST BE JOKING, BY HERMES!

WHERE DO YOU THINK YOU ARE?
I KNOW WHERE I AM ALL RIGHT. WHAT I WANT TO KNOW IS WHETHER IT'S WORTH STAYING

TWO AND A HALF SESTERTII, I SAID!
FOUR!

HE SAYS TWO SESTERTII IS THE MAXIMUM PRICE FOR THIS CLASS OF HOTEL
?!

HOW MUCH IS THAT IN NEW PENCE?
NEW PENCE? WELL NOW, THAT COMES TO...

LOOK, ARE WE GOING TO HANG AROUND HERE ALL DAY? WHAT ABOUT THIS TRAINING, BY TOUTATIS, OR DO YOU WANT US TO LODGE A COMPLAINT?

SOON AFTERWARDS...
YOU CERTAINLY TOOK YOUR TIME, NEFARIUS PURPUS! WELL, SO THESE ARE THE NEW LEGIONARIES?
FUNNY SORT OF CHAP, OUR CENTURION!

YERRRRSSSS!
YOU KNOW WHAT'S WRONG WITH HIM? IF YOU ASK ME, HE'S IN LOVE!

I... I'LL GO AND WAIT FOR YOU IN THE CENTURIONS' MESS...
NOW, YOU LISTEN TO ME, YOU BARBAROUS LOT! I'M YOUR INSTRUCTOR, I AM! IT'S MY JOB TO MAKE LEGIONARIES OF YOU...

FINE, BUT GET ON WITH IT! WE'RE IN A HURRY!
WHAT?

SILENCE IN THE RANKS! NOBODY BAT AN EYELID! I'LL BREAK YOU IN, BY JUPITER!

DON'T TALK SO FAST! I CAN'T KEEP UP WITH THE TRANSLATION
SHUT UP!
TAN TANTARA

AS FOR YOU, CLEVER...
SSH! CAN'T YOU SEE YOU'RE DISTURBING THE POOR TRUMPETER?
TANTAN TARA

TANTAN TARA
GRUB'S UP!
JUST IN THE NICK OF TIME! I'M HUNGRY!
GRUB?
Grub

IN THE CENTURIONS' MESS...

HELLO THERE, DUBIUS STATUS. TAKEN YOUR NEW RECRUITS IN HAND?

YERRRSSS!
IN LOVE, IS HE?
19

THE EGYPTIAN WANTS TO SEE THE MENU
I SAY, DO YOU THINK THEY'LL HAVE BOAR?
DON'T GET ANY IDEAS! THE STRONGER THE ARMY, THE WORSE ITS FOOD IS. THAT'S WHAT KEEPS THE MEN IN A NASTY MOOD!

FLOTCH!

PLOTCH!
SLOP!

FLOTCH!
I DIDN'T THINK THE ROMAN ARMY WAS THAT STRONG!

THE EGYPTIAN WANTS TO SEE THE MANAGER
I'M NOT STAYING FOR LESS THAN SIX SESTERTII A DAY!
POSITIVELY GOTHIC, THIS FOOD!
At home people would be quartered for less!
BANG!

LOOK, NO JOKING... WHAT IS IT?
IT'S LEGIONARY RATIONS... YOU'LL BE GETTING IT EVERY DAY. CORN, BACON AND CHEESE, ALL COOKED TOGETHER TO SAVE TIME!

LET'S GO AND HAVE A WORD WITH THE COOK, ASTERIX!
JUST WHAT I WAS ABOUT TO SUGGEST MYSELF, OBELIX!
SLOUP! SLOUP!

DELICIOUS! REALLY SPLENDID, DON'T YOU KNOW!

HEY! ARE YOU THE COOK AROUND HERE?
?

WHAT ARE YOU DOING HERE, BY VESTA?
LET ME TALK TO HIM, ASTERIX!

I'M AFRAID WE DON'T THINK MUCH OF YOUR FOOD
HOHOHOHO!

I SUPPOSE YOU'D LIKE SOME FANCY COOKING?
THAT'S RIGHT! WILD BOAR!
AND PLENTY OF IT! WE NEED ALL THE STRENGTH WE CAN GET!

FANCY CAKES TOO? I BET YOU LIKE FANCY CAKES?
HM... WHAT DO YOU THINK, OBELIX? HOW ABOUT A FEW CAKES?
YES! OH, YES!

YOU GET OUT, OR I'LL HAVE YOU IN THE COOLER!

CAN I BE POLITE TO HIM, ASTERIX?
!
GO RIGHT AHEAD, OBELIX!

BAFFF!
TERRIBLY SORRY

SPLOSH!
NOW, ROMAN, LISTEN TO ME! ANY TIME WE'RE NOT SATISFIED WITH OUR FOOD WE'LL BE PAYING YOU ANOTHER VISIT! COME ON OBELIX!

HAVE THEY GONE?
YES

RIGHT! YOU'D BETTER GO TO MARKET TO BUY WILD BOAR AND FLOUR AND EGGS AND SUGAR AND CRYSTALLIZED FRUITS. BEFORE YOU GO, PUT OUT THE FIRE UNDER MY CAULDRON

RIGHT! YOU'VE BEEN ASSIGNED TO THE 1ST LEGION, 3RD COHORT, 2ND MANIPLE, 1ST CENTURY. YOU HAVE TO REPEAT THAT WHEN PRESENTING YOURSELVES TO A SUPERIOR OFFICER!
THAT COOK IS CRAZY!
DID YOU REALLY ENJOY YOUR LUNCH?
YES, RATHER!

YOU, SHORTIE! PRESENT YOURSELF!
WHAT?

OH... ASTERIX THE GAUL!

AND I'M OBELIX! THE OTHERS ARE OUR PALS. WHAT'S YOUR NAME?
INSTRUCTOR DUBIUS STATUS, 1ST LEGION, 3RD COHORT...

GRRR... GET BACK INTO LINE, WILL YOU... GRR... GET BACK!
22A

NOW WE DO PILUM DRILL. YOU TRY TO HIT THAT TARGET AT THE OTHER SIDE OF THE SQUARE. YOU START, LEGIONARY OBELIX

RIGHT!

TCHOC!

COOKHOUSE

ALL RIGHT, ALL RIGHT, ALL RIGHT! JUST GIVE ME TIME TO COOK THE BOARS, WILL YOU?
22B

ER... NOW WE HAVE GLADIUS DRILL...

THESE ARE ONLY PRETEND SWORDS, OF COURSE, MADE OF WOOD... COME ON!
?!

WELL, COME ON! DEFEND YOURSELF!
BUT IF IT'S ONLY MADE OF WOOD...

DO AS YOU'RE TOLD, OBELIX! WE'RE ONLY WASTING TIME!!
OH, VERY WELL!

THESE ROMANS ARE CRAZY!
TCHAC!

OH NO! IF THIS GOES ON IT'LL NEVER BE READY, AND IT'LL TASTE PRETTY FUNNY TOO!
23A

THAT EVENING...
CHEER UP, DUBIUS STATUS! THE RECRUITS WILL HAVE TO BE UP AT THE CRACK OF DAWN FOR A ROUTE MARCH WITH SACKS FULL OF ROCKS. THAT'LL KEEP THEM QUIET...

JUST A SHOT OF MAGIC POTION FOR TOMORROW, AND I'M TURNING IN. WE HAVE TO BE UP EARLY!
MORE BOAR HERE!
COMING!

THAT'S A NICE THOUGHT! THEY WON'T BE QUITE SO SMART WHEN I GET THEM OUT OF BED AT DAWN TOMORROW!

BUT ONLY A FEW SHORT HOURS LATER...
WAKEY, WAAAKEY!
?

RISE AND SHINE!
COME ON EVERY-ONE!
C-C-COMING!
23B

SO THOSE BARBARIANS ARE IN A HURRY? THEY'LL SOON CHANGE THEIR TUNE, BY JUPITER!

EVERY MAN TO A SACK! AND JUMP TO IT, BY MERCURY!

WHO'S HE CALLING?
A PORTER

THAT'S ENOUGH OF THAT! GET MOVING!

He says the staff at this hotel should be given the sack!
24A

BELENOS, APOLLO AND RA ARE NOT KIND, AND THE SUN BEATS DOWN ON THE NEW LEGIONARIES...
WE CAN'T GO ON LIKE THIS!
WE CERTAINLY CAN'T!
AHA! LESS FOOLING AROUND NOW, EH? DRAGGING OUR FEET NOW, ARE WE? LOST OUR VIS COMICA, HMM?

DON'T YOU WORRY. WE'LL FIX IT FOR YOU!
OR IT'LL TAKE ALL DAY!
?!

HEY! HAND US YOUR SACKS, YOU LOT!
WHAT THE...?

AT THE DOUBLE NOW... WE'RE WANTED IN AFRICA, WE ARE!
SO THE SOONER WE'RE THROUGH WITH THESE SILLY EXERCISES THE BETTER!
24B

WAIT A MINUTE! WAIT A MINUTE! THAT'S NOT THE IDEA AT ALL!

DO YOU WANT THESE SACKS CARRIED OR DON'T YOU?

?!?
WELL, COME ON THEN!!!

SOME HOURS LATER...
DUBIUS STATUS AND HIS MEN WILL SOON BE BACK. I CAN'T WAIT TO SEE WHAT SORT OF STATE THEY'RE IN...

?!?

WHAT THE...?
THEY...THEY CARRIED ALL THE SACKS! THEY TOOK IT IN TURNS TO CARRY THEIR MATES AND THEY RAN...AND...

...I CAN'T TAKE ANY MORE!
THERE, THERE! THE TRAINING'S OVER...
POF! POF!

MEN OF THE 1ST LEGION, 3RD COHORT, 2ND MANIPLE, 1ST CENTURY! WE'RE LEAVING FOR MASSILIA AT ONCE. CAESAR AWAITS US! I AM SURE YOU ARE EAGER TO GO INTO BATTLE AND...

COME ON, THEN! LET'S GET OUR THINGS!
?
What did the centurion say?
I'll tell you some other time

YOU CAN STOP LAUGHING, IDIOT! YOU'RE COMING TOO ...AND SO'S THE COOK!

UNDER THE COMMAND OF CENTURION NEFARIUS PURPUS, THE MEN OF THE 1ST LEGION, 3RD COHORT, 2ND MANIPLE, 1ST CENTURY, LEAVE CONDATUM...

I THINK WE'VE BEEN GOING LONG ENOUGH... WE'LL STOP FOR A BIT...

1ST LEGION, 3RD COHORT, 2ND MANIPLE, 1ST CENTURY, HALT! WE'RE HAVING A BREAK!

THE QUICKER WE FIND TRAGICOMIX THE BETTER FOR PANACEA...
I DON'T WANT HER TO WORRY...
26A

D'YOU THINK IT'LL BE EASY TO FIND TRAGICOMIX?
HEY! YOU TWO! I SAID WE'RE HAVING A BREAK!
LET'S HOPE SO OBELIX!

NO TIME! COME ON! COME ON!
BUT I'M GIVING THE ORDERS AROUND HERE! THIS IS A BREAK! HEY, THIS IS A BREAK...

YOU GO AHEAD! WE'RE GOING ON!

THAT WAS A GOOD ONE, THAT WAS!
WELL, HOW'S THIS FOR ATTIC SALT? OUR CENTURION'S ZEUSLESS!
THAT'D LAY THEM IN THE ISLES, OLD BOY!
I'm not sure just how to put that in Gothic and Egyptian, but I'll do my best...
!!!

CRAZY! THEY'RE CRAZY! THEY'RE ACTUALLY EAGER TO GO INTO BATTLE!
26B
PAF!

THE COLUMN OF THE 1ST LEGION, 3RD COHORT, 2ND MANIPLE, 1ST CENTURY IS STILL ON THE GO, BUT HAS UNDERGONE A SLIGHT MODIFICATION AS TO MARCHING ORDER...

HALT! WE'LL CAMP HERE FOR TONIGHT!

ER...UM...RIGHT! DIG A DITCH ROUND THE SITE... BUILD A STOCKADE! PITCH YOUR TENTS AROUND YOUR CENTURION'S TENT! ORGANISE SENTRY DUTY...

I SHOULDN'T BOTHER. LOOK AT 'EM!
POF!
POF!

!!!
TONIGHT'S MENU: BOAR ON THE SPIT AND GÂTEAU À LA CRÈME
SUITS ME!
I'LL HAVE MY BOAR MEDIUM RARE, PLEASE

WHILE THEIR MEN ARE STUFFING THEMSELVES, THE TWO ROMAN OFFICERS MAKE DO WITH THE FRUGAL REGULATION MEAL IN THEIR SMALL REGULATION TENT...
HONK!
SCRONTCH!
SLOP!SLIP!
SCRITCH MIAM!

AFTER A SHORT NIGHT'S SLEEP...
YAWN!

?

NEFARIUS PURPUS! THEY'VE GONE!

GONE! HOW DO YOU MEAN, GONE?
WITH BAG AND BAGGAGE, THAT'S HOW!

WHAT ABOUT THE TENT...?
TO PLUTO WITH THE TENT! LET'S GET AFTER THEM!

THERE THEY ARE!
WAIT FOR US! YOOHOO! WAIT FOR US!

WHAT THE...??? WHAT ARE YOU DOING IN CIVVIES?
IT'S BETTER FOR MARCHING...
...AND MORE FETCHING!

THEY MAKE RAPID PROGRESS, IN PLEASANT STAGES...
DINNER IS SERVED!

AT LAST THEY REACH MASSILIA, THE GREAT PORT WHERE TROOPS EMBARK FOR AFRICA
LEGIONARY! WHERE'S THE LEGIONARY H.Q.?
VIII
MASSILIA

WHO ARE YOU, THEN?

CENTURION NEFARIUS PURPUS AND THE MEN OF THE 1ST LEGION, 3RD COHORT, 2ND MANIPLE, 1ST CENTURY!
?!

THE BARRACKS ARE IN THE NEW PORT. JUST A WORD OF ADVICE, BY JUPITER! GET YOURSELVES SMARTENED UP! IF YOU GO ABOUT MASSILIA DRESSED UP LIKE THAT YOU'LL SOON GET A DRESSING DOWN!

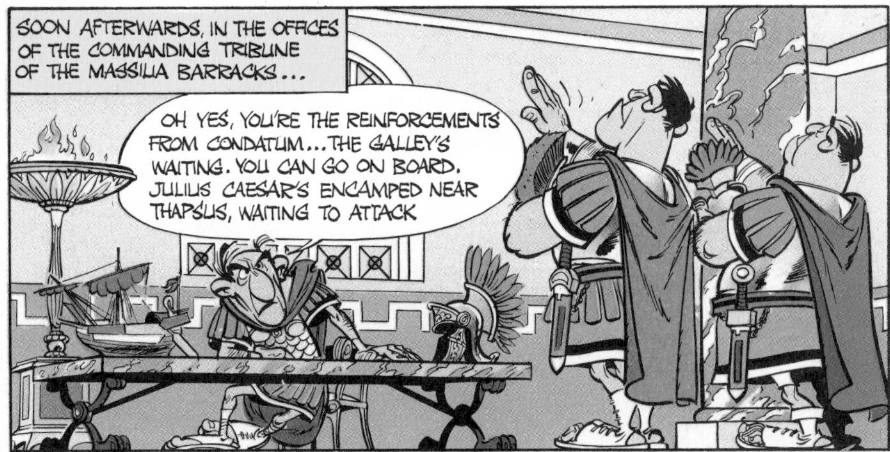
SOON AFTERWARDS, IN THE OFFICES OF THE COMMANDING TRIBUNE OF THE MASSILIA BARRACKS...
OH YES, YOU'RE THE REINFORCEMENTS FROM CONDATUM... THE GALLEY'S WAITING. YOU CAN GO ON BOARD. JULIUS CAESAR'S ENCAMPED NEAR THAPSUS, WAITING TO ATTACK

HERE'S OUR GALLEY!
KEEP RANKS! KEEP QUIET... PLEASE KEEP QUIET!

CENTURION NEFARIUS PURPUS, READY TO LEAVE WHEN THE TIDE ALLOWS!
29A

WHAT DID THAT MAN SAY?
OLD HAIRY EYEBROWS

HAHAHA HA!
I SEE! WE'RE A FEW OARSMEN SHORT. EXERCISE WILL KEEP THEM QUIET!
NOTHING WILL KEEP THIS LOT QUIET, CAPTAIN ... NOTHING WILL KEEP THEM QUIET!

LET GO AFT!

WH... WHAT D'YOU MEAN, LET GO AFT?
THERE SHE GOES!

HE SAID...
I KNOW, I KNOW... OLD HAIRY NOSE
29B

CRUISING DOWN THE RIVER ON A SUNDAY AFTERNOON
I SAY, HOW ABOUT A BOAT RACE, WHAT?
NEVER ON SUNDAY!
ALL ROWS LEAD TO ROME... GET IT? ALL ROWS LEAD TO ROME!
?
!!?

THINK YOU'RE CLEVER, EH? I'LL SOON SETTLE YOUR HASH. YOU THERE! SPEED UP THE STROKE!
THAT'S WHAT THE LITTLE GAUL ALREADY TOLD ME...I'M GIVING HER ALL I'VE GOT!
BONG! BONG! BONG

BUT NOT FAR AWAY...
SAIL TO STARBOARD, CAP'N!
HOW MANY?

ONLY ONE, CAP'N, AND NOT TOO BIG!
SURE SHE'S ROMAN? NO GAULS? WE DON'T WANT TO SAIL TOO NEAR THE WIND

THEY'RE ALL IN ROMAN UNIFORM... WE CAN TAKE THE WIND OUT OF THEIR SAILS!
SURE?

SURE! THEY'LL SOON BE OUT OF THEIR DEPTH!
RIGHT! STAND BY TO BOARD! HARRGH HARRGH HARRGH!

AND ABOARD THE ROMAN GALLEY THEY'RE GETTING WORRIED...
PIRATE SHIP TO PORT!
HMM! SHE LOOKS STRONG. I THINK WE'LL TAKE EVASIVE ACTION

HARD A-PORT!
HARD A-PORT!

LOOK, ONCE AND FOR ALL, WHO'S GIVING THE COMMANDS?
OLD HAIRY HANDS!

THAT GALLEY'S COMING RIGHT FOR US, CAP'N!
RIGHT FOR US? THEN THEY'RE ON BOARD! DON'T ASK ME HOW OR WHY... I JUST KNOW THEY'RE ON BOARD! LET'S GET OUT OF HERE!

LET'S GET...
TOO LATE!
HOW'S THINGS?

SOON AFTERWARDS...
WE'VE BEEN FRAMED, BY JERICHO!*
*ANCIENT GAULISH ARTIST

MEANWHILE, THE ROMAN GALLEY CONTINUES ON ITS WAY...
CRAZY! THEY'RE CRAZY!
CAPTAIN, YOU'RE TELLING ME!

AFTER A FEW MORE DAYS AT SEA...
HERE WE ARE. THAT'S THE COAST OF AFRICA... I'M JUST GOING TO HAVE A WORD WITH YOUR MEN...

LOOK, WILL YOU LET ME BRING HER IN? PROMISE? THEN YOU'LL ALL GET YOUR TOT OF RUM...

AND IF THAT EGYPTIAN SAYS ANOTHER HIEROGLYPHIC I, PERSONALLY, WILL THROW HIM OVERBOARD!!!

AT LAST THE REINFORCEMENTS LAND ON AFRICAN SOIL...
BE SEEING YOU!
OH NO! OH NO!
WE MUST JOIN CAESAR'S LEGIONS RIGHT AWAY. THEY'RE ENCAMPED NEAR THAPSUS

QUO VADIS?
WE'RE THE REINFORCEMENTS! 1ST LEGION, 3RD COHORT, 2ND MANIPLE, 1ST CENTURY!

THE CENTURION OF THE WATCH WILL SHOW YOU TO YOUR QUARTERS
WE'LL GO AND LOOK FOR TRAGICOMIX AT ONCE, SO WE CAN GET HOME TO GAUL AS SOON AS POSSIBLE
YES, LET'S! THE SOONER WE SCARAB OFF THE BETTER! *
He says it's a very nice holiday camp
* THESE DAYS WE SHOULD SAY 'BEETLE'

1ST LEGION, 3RD COHORT, 2ND MANIPLE, 1ST CENTURY, TAKING UP ITS QUARTERS!
REALLY? WHERE IS THE 1ST LEGION, 3RD COHORT, 2ND MANIPLE, 1ST CENTURY, THEN?

?!?
THE TWO GAULS HAVE GONE TO LOOK FOR A FRIEND, THE GREEK FOUND SOME MEN PLAYING DICE, THE BELGIAN, THE BRITON AND THE GOTH WENT TO HAVE A BEER, THE COOK'S LOOKING FOR INGREDIENTS FOR CRÊPES SUZETTE, AND DUBIUS STATUS HAS REPORTED SICK. MAY I FALL OUT NOW?

THERE, THERE, YOU'LL SOON BE SEEING YOUR GIRL AGAIN!
32

JULIUS CAESAR'S TENT...
SCIPIO IS LYING IN WAIT TO THE NORTH, JUBA 1ST, KING OF NUMIDIA, AND THE TRAITOR AFRANIUS TO THE SOUTH. WE CAN THEREFORE SEE THAT OUR POSITION...

?

WHO ARE YOU ? HOW DARE YOU ENTER CAESAR'S TENT ?
ARE YOU THERE, PTENISNET ?

WHAT'S THIS MAN SAYING ?
HE...ER, HE WANTS TO KNOW IF YOU'RE ONE OF THE REDCLOAKS...ER, ONE OF THE HOLIDAY CAMP HELPERS...WHAT SORT OF ACTIVITIES YOU...ER...

GET OUT!

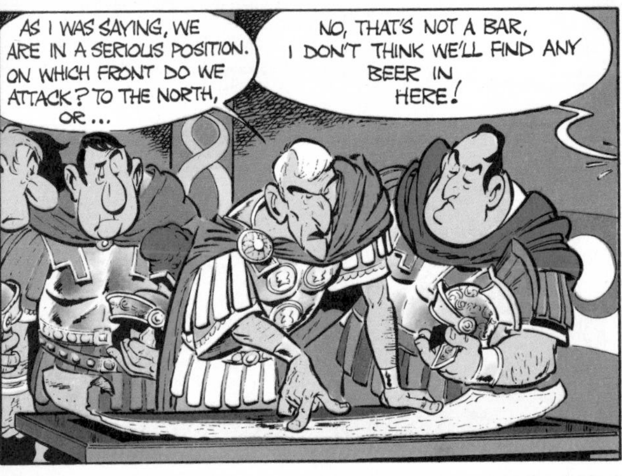
AS I WAS SAYING, WE ARE IN A SERIOUS POSITION. ON WHICH FRONT DO WE ATTACK ? TO THE NORTH, OR...
NO, THAT'S NOT A BAR, I DON'T THINK WE'LL FIND ANY BEER IN HERE!

AWFULLY SORRY! WE SAW THIS BIG TENT, AND WE THOUGHT IT MIGHT BE...
GET OUT, BY JUPITER!!!

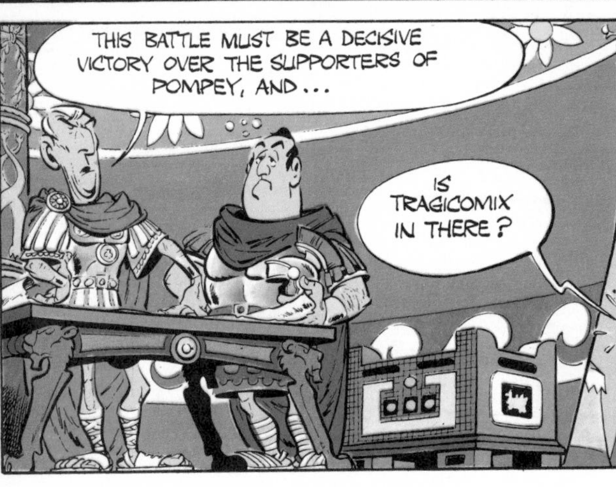
THIS BATTLE MUST BE A DECISIVE VICTORY OVER THE SUPPORTERS OF POMPEY, AND...
IS TRAGICOMIX IN THERE ?

WHO THE DEVIL ARE ALL THESE PEOPLE ?

1ST LEGION, 3RD COHORT, 2ND MANIPLE, 1ST CENTURY. AVE!

SO THERE YOU ARE! THINGS ARE GOING TO BE A BIT DIFFERENT HERE! THIS IS A MILITARY CAMP! THERE'S GOT TO BE DISCIPLINE HERE! THEY'VE GOT A GUARDROOM HERE! AND I KNOW SOMEONE WHO...

OFFICER IN COMMAND OF THE DETACHMENT OF THE 1ST LEGION, 3RD COHORT, 2ND MANIPLE, 1ST CENTURY?
THAT'S RIGHT!

RIGHT! WE ARREST YOU IN THE NAME OF JULIUS CAESAR, WHO DOESN'T LIKE BEING INTERRUPTED WHEN HE'S TALKING! IT'S THE GUARDROOM FOR YOU!

WE'VE BEEN LOOKING FOR TRAGICOMIX ALL OVER THE PLACE, AND WE CAN'T FIND HIM ANYWHERE...
HE MUST BE SOMEWHERE IN AFRICA!

AVE, ROOKIES! COME FOR A BIT OF ACTIVE SERVICE? I COULD GIVE YOU A SPOT OF ADVICE IF THERE WAS SOME FREE DRINK GOING!

I'M AN OLD HAND OUT HERE. I KNOW MY WAY AROUND! I KNOW EVERYBODY, I DO!
BONG! BONG! BONG!
DO YOU KNOW A LEGIONARY CALLED TRAGICOMIX?

TRAGICOMIX... TRAGICOMIX WITH A T, AS IN TIMEO DANAOS ET DONA FERENTES?

YOUNG FELLOW? GOOD LOOKING?
YES, THAT'S HIM!
WELL, NOT ALL THAT GOOD-LOOKING!

POOR CHAP! HE'D ONLY JUST GOT HERE WHEN HE WAS LOST IN A SKIRMISH WITH SCIPIO'S MEN...
34

YOU MEAN TRAGICOMIX HAS BEEN...
WELL, MAYBE NOT. THEY DO SOMETIMES TAKE PRISONERS FOR QUESTIONING

YOU MIGHT FIND OUT MORE WHEN H2SO4 GETS BACK TONIGHT
H2SO4 ?

YES, HE'S OUR TOP SPY. HE'S GONE TO FIND OUT WHAT SCIPIO'S DOING. I'LL BRING HIM OVER WHEN HE COMES BACK, HE'S A FRIEND OF MINE

FUNNY SORT OF NAME, H2SO4
THAT'S HIS CODE NAME. HIS REAL NAME IS VITRIOLIX... HOW ABOUT THAT DRINK, THEN ?

GO ROUND TO OUR COOK'S TENT...
TELL HIM WE SENT YOU
THANKS, PALS! SEE YOU TONIGHT

THAT NIGHT, OUTSIDE THE CAMP GATES...
GIVE THE PASSWORD!
H2SO4

DIGNUS EST INTRARE
PASS, FRIEND!

CAESAR'S EXPECTING YOU, H2SO4

SCIPIO IS MAKING PREPARATIONS TO ATTACK, O CAESAR. HE HAS A POWERFUL ARMY
HMM... I OUGHT TO ATTACK FIRST, BUT I WONDER, I WONDER...

SOME ROOKIES WANT TO TALK TO YOU, H2SO4. THE BOOZE THEY'VE GOT IN THEIR TENT! IT'S GREAT!
I'M WITH YOU, GARRULUS VINUS!

YES, I DID SEE SOME PRISONERS IN SCIPIO'S CAMP... YES, TRAGICOMIX THE GAUL WAS THERE... THE GOOD-LOOKING ONE...
HUH!

WHERE IS SCIPIO'S CAMP?
TO THE NORTH. YOU CAN'T MISS IT. ONCE THEY MASSCRE YOU, YOU'RE THERE

HAVE SOME REFRESHMENTS. I THINK THERE'S SOME SEAFOOD SOUFFLÉ LEFT
SEAFOOD SOUFFLÉ??!
GREAT, I TOLD YOU... REALLY GREAT!

AS FOR US, WE'RE OFF TO RESCUE TRAGICOMIX!
WHAT, THE GOOD-LOOKING ONE?

OBELIX, THIS IS NO TIME TO BE JEALOUS! REMEMBER YOUR PROMISE TO PANACEA!
OH, ALL RIGHT... HE MUST BE A BIT OF A NITWIT, THOUGH, IF HE GETS HIMSELF CAPTURED BY THE ROMANS!

HE DIDN'T HAVE ANY MAGIC POTION!
SO WHAT...

HE'S STILL A GOOD-LOOKING NITWIT
GLUG GLUG GLUG!

AND NOW TO GET OUT OF THE CAMP!
I DIDN'T KNOW WE WERE ALLOWED OUT AT NIGHT

HALT! GIVE THE PASSWORD!
BUT THE PASSWORD'S FOR COMING IN. WE'RE GOING OUT!

ER... JUST A MINUTE. I'LL GO AND ASK THE CENTURION...
THAT'S RIGHT. WE'RE LAW-ABIDING ROMAN LEGIONARIES, WE ARE!
WE ROMANS ARE CRAZY!
TAP! TAP! TAP!

CRACK!
NOW, LET'S NOT WASTE ANY MORE TIME!

AND NOT FAR AWAY, ONE OF CAESAR'S PATROLS, SENT TO FIND OUR GAULISH FRIENDS...

CHARGE! CHARGE!
OH, SIMMER DOWN, SIMMER DOWN! SCIPIO'S CAMP IS JUST OVER THERE. YOU'LL HAVE RAISED THE ALARM WITH ALL THAT ROW

NEVER MIND! LET'S STRIKE NOW!
I CALL THAT CUNNING STRATEGY!

MEANWHILE, IN CAESAR'S CAMP...
SCIPIO'S ATTACKING? HE'S FORCING MY HAND... PERHAPS IT'S ALL FOR THE BEST! WE'LL ATTACK!

ALEA JACTA EST, AS I ALWAYS SAY

AND OUTSIDE SCIPIO'S CAMP...
GIVE THE PASSWORD!
OPEN UP!
BONG! BONG! BONG!
38A

DO YOU REMEMBER IT, OBELIX?
YOU KNOW WHAT I'M LIKE WITH FOREIGN LANGUAGES... ANYWAY, YOU'RE MUCH BETTER AT THINKING AND SUMMING THINGS UP

NEVER MIND!
OI!
IT'S FUN OPENING GATES THIS WAY, ISN'T IT?
BONG!

YOU CAN'T COME IN! LOOK HERE, YOU CAN'T COME IN!
OH, YES, WE CAN!

TCHONG!
STOP... HANG ON!

I'VE GOT IT! COGITO, ERGO SUM...

TO ARMS! WE'RE BEING ATTACKED! SOUND THE ALARM!
YOU LIKE PLENTY OF ROMANS, OBELIX. YOU'VE GOT A PLATEFUL COMING!
WELL, YOU KNOW ROMANS ARE LIKE OYSTERS... YOU CAN HAVE TOO MUCH OF A GOOD THING
38B

DO YOU THINK CAESAR'S THROWING THE FULL WEIGHT OF HIS TROOPS AGAINST US?
I DON'T WEIGH THAT MUCH!
STOP ARGUING, OBELIX, AND TRY TO FIND OUT WHERE THE PRISONERS ARE
WHUMPH!
TCHAC!

PAF!
IT'S NO GOOD, ASTERIX. THEY WON'T ANSWER BEFORE YOU HIT THEM AND THEY CAN'T ANSWER AFTERWARDS

TO ARMS! THAT WAS ONLY THE ADVANCE PARTY! THE WHOLE ARMY IS ATTACKING US NOW!
NOW THE FAT'S REALLY IN THE FIRE...
WHO SAID FAT!?

O SCIPIO, JULIUS CAESAR'S ARMY IS ATTACKING US!
VERY WELL, WE'LL GO OUT TO MEET IT! DOWN WITH THE USURPER! LET'S MAKE A SORTIE!

CHARGE!
LET'S GET AT THEM!
LET'S GET OUT OF HERE!
WHAT ABOUT US, THEN?
IF YOU DON'T MIND... I'VE SORT OF GOT TO MAKE A SORTIE...

ONE LAST WORD... WHERE ARE THE PRISONERS?
IN THE ENCLOSURE OVER THERE... DO LET GO NOW. THEY'RE WAITING FOR ME

IS TRAGICOMIX HERE?
THAT'S ME

WE'VE COME TO LOOK FOR YOU. PANACEA SENT US
HOW WONDERFUL! THANK YOU, THANK YOU, THANK YOU!
DON'T MENTION IT!

BUT DO YOU THINK THEY'LL LET US OUT?
OF COURSE THEY WILL!
ASTERIX, CAN I HAVE A WORD WITH YOU?

WHAT IS IT?
DO YOU HONESTLY THINK HE'S ALL THAT GOOD-LOOKING?

WHAT ON EARTH'S HAPPENING? THE CAMP'S DESERTED!
IT'S ONLY THE ROMANS FIGHTING EACH OTHER...NOTHING TO DO WITH US
IDIOT? WHAT DID HE MEAN, IDIOT?

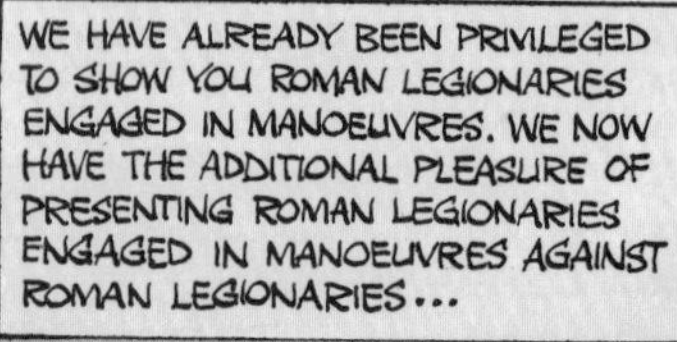
WE HAVE ALREADY BEEN PRIVILEGED TO SHOW YOU ROMAN LEGIONARIES ENGAGED IN MANOEUVRES. WE NOW HAVE THE ADDITIONAL PLEASURE OF PRESENTING ROMAN LEGIONARIES ENGAGED IN MANOEUVRES AGAINST ROMAN LEGIONARIES...

FORM A PHALANX!
FORM A SQUARE!
FORM A QUINCUNX!
FORM A CIRCLE!

FORM A TORTOISE!

WAIT A MINUTE! DON'T KNOW YOU, DO I?
HEY, ISN'T THIS CAESAR'S TORTOISE?
NO IT ISN'T!
YES IT IS!

HE WANTS TO KNOW WHAT'S GOING ON
TELL HIM THEY'RE AS CONFUSED AS HE IS!

COME ON, MEN! FORWARD!
BUT WE'RE NOT YOUR MEN!
HEY! THOSE ARE MY MEN!

FINALLY SCIPIO, HEARTILY SICK OF THE WHOLE AFFAIR, SIGNALS THE RETREAT. JULIUS CAESAR HAS WON!
IT'S NOT FAIR! I'M OFF! SOUND THE RETREAT!
I ONLY TAKE ORDERS FROM CAESAR!
OH, SHUT UP! HE'S TALKING TO ME!
40

LET'S FETCH OUR THINGS FROM CAESAR'S CAMP AND GET BACK TO GAUL
HOW SIMPLE EVERYTHING SEEMS WITH YOU!
THAT'S BECAUSE WE USE OUR HEADS!

SOON AFTERWARDS...
HOW IS MY DARLING LITTLE PANACEA?
SHE'S ALL RIGHT

LOOK! CAESAR'S ARMY IS COMING BACK!
WHAT DO WE DO?
WHAT DO WE DO...?

WE CHARGE, BY TOUTATIS!
41A

OBELIX!
SOMEBODY WANTS YOU!
CRAAASH!

WELL, WHAT IS IT?
THERE'S NO POINT IN GETTING WORKED UP. HERE COMES JULIUS CAESAR!

I SEEM TO HAVE SEEN YOU SOMEWHERE BEFORE, GAULS. WHO ARE YOU?
OBELIX AND ASTERIX!
1ST LEGION, 3RD COHORT AND I CAN'T REMEMBER THE REST

WE SIGNED ON IN YOUR ARMY TO GET TRAGICOMIX BACK FOR PANACEA!
41B

OH, SO IT WAS YOU WHO STARTED THIS BATTLE WHEN YOU LEFT MY CAMP?
BATTLE? WHAT BATTLE?

I KNOW YOU ARE MY ENEMIES, GAULS, BUT TODAY YOU HAVE BROUGHT ME VICTORY. CAESAR IS NOT UNGRATEFUL! I WILL GRANT ANY FAVOUR YOU CARE TO ASK!

WE'D LIKE TO GO HOME, JULIUS.
GRANTED!
I'M GOING TO SEE PANACEA AGAIN! I'M GOING TO SEE PANACEA AGAIN!
?

THE TIME HAS COME TO SAY GOODBYE...
YOU HAVE BROUGHT GLORY TO THE 1ST LEGION, 3RD COHORT, 2ND MANIPLE, 1ST CENTURY!
NO HARD FEELINGS, NEFARIUS PURPUS!
WE'LL NEVER FORGET YOU!
I SAY!
BY ZEUS!
He says all this camaraderie reminds him of when he was in the army!
These Egyptians are crazy!
I'M GOING TO SEE PANACEA AGAIN! I'M GOING TO SEE PANACEA AGAIN!
42A

OFF WE GO! THE GALLEY CAESAR HAS LENT US IS WAITING
I'M GOING TO SEE PANACEA AGAIN! I'M GOING TO SEE PANACEA AGAIN!
NYAHNYAHNYAH!

SOON AFTERWARDS...
OH NO! NOT THEM!

LET GO AFT!
THERE SHE GOES!

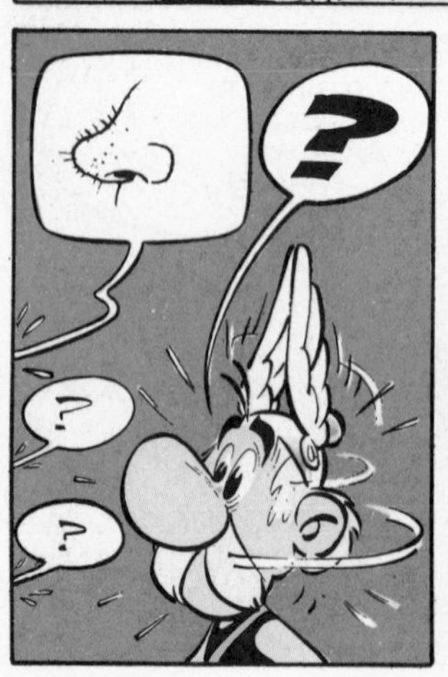
?
?
?

42B

AND WHILE THE ROMAN GALLEY BEARS OUR FRIENDS HOME TOWARDS THE PLEASANT SHORES OF GAUL, THERE IS AN ENEMY STANDING OUT TO SEA, WATCHING AND WAITING...
LUCKY THING WE MANAGED TO BUY THIS SHIP FROM THE PHOENICIANS WHO PICKED US UP OFF THE RAFT! BUT IT COST A LOT OF MONEY... WE MUST PAY THE INSTALMENTS OFF FAST...

SHIP FULL AHEAD, CAP'N!
SPLENDID! THIS WILL KEEP OUR HEADS ABOVE WATER!

FOLLOW ME, ME HEARTIES! HIP HIP...

HURRAY!

AT LAST, AFTER AN ALMOST UNEVENTFUL VOYAGE, WE RETURN IN TRIUMPH TO THE GAULISH VILLAGE...

PANACEA!
DOGMATIX!

OH, THANK YOU, THANK YOU! HOW CAN I EVER THANK YOU?
IT WAS NOTHING, REALLY...

NOTHING? YOU MUST BE JOKING! YOU SHOULD HAVE SEEN THEM, PANACEA! THEY WERE GREAT! FANTASTIC! OBELIX ATTACKED CAESAR'S ARMY ALL BY HIMSELF!
OH, WELL, IT WAS JUST A LITTLE ARMY YOU KNOW...

the end

PRINTED IN BELGIUM BY proost INTERNATIONAL BOOK PRODUCTION